Originally published in Dutch as *Door de bril van Bill* in the series "De Lettertuin," copyright © 1997 by Bakermat Uitgevers, Mechelen, Belgium. All rights reserved.

Published in the U.S. in 2002 by Big Tent Entertainment, 216 West 18th Street, New York, New York 10011.

ISBN: 1-59226-049-7

Printed in China.

Listening to Stories

By
Marleen Wynants

Through Bill's Glasses

Illustrated by
Vero Beauprez

BIG TENT ENTERTAINMENT

My name is Bill.
I am writing a book
about my life.
It's full of people I know
and things I do.

This is the world
through my glasses!

My Mom

I have a sweet tooth.
My mom wishes I wouldn't eat
so much candy.

"Not until after dinner!"
she cries.
Oops! It's too late.
My hand is empty,
and my mouth is full.

Mom plays the bass.
All day long I hear
doop, doop, doop.
Mom is good.
But sometimes
she plays too loud,
and the neighbor calls to
complain.
Doop, doop, doop.

Whenever I'm sad,
Mom makes me laugh.

"Look, I can blow up
my belly like a balloon!"
she says.
I laugh and laugh.

"Stop, Mom," I call.
My jaw hurts
from laughing so much.

My Dad

My dad is cool.
Sometimes he pretends
he's a dragon,
and I play a hero.
My dad is a good dragon
because he's so tall.

"Much too tall,"
says Mom.
"Come here.
I will make you shorter."

Snip! Snip!
She cuts dad's hair very short.
Poor dragon!

My Sister

My sister has curly hair,
but I don't.
I wear glasses,
but my sister doesn't.
Sometimes she puts on
my glasses.
"Help!" she says.
"I can't see a thing!"

After she takes them off,
she pretends she still can't see.
"Where's my doll?" she cries.
"I can't find my doll!"

My sister is ten.
She says she's eleven.
She likes ice cream.
And she likes Dean, too.
She doesn't like
doing her chores.
Sometimes I do them for her—
but only when she
gives me candy!

My Tree House

Drip.
There is a hole in the roof
of my tree house.
"Dad," I yell.
"Come here quick!"

Dad looks around.
He plugs the holes
with his pinkie and his thumb.
The roof stops leaking.
But now Dad can't move!
"I hope it stops raining soon,"
he says.

My Class

The kids in my class
act wild sometimes.
Ben is on top of the cabinet.
Carol is throwing paper airplanes.

Brriiing!
As soon as the bell rings,
everything changes.
The kids race to their desks.

"Ben, what's two times three?"
asks the teacher.
Ben doesn't know.
The teacher calls on Bess.
"Two times three is six,"
answers Bess.
"Well done, Bess,"
the teacher says.

Bess smiles.
She has a hole in her mouth
where a tooth used to be.
Bess makes me blush.
I don't want the class to see,
so I pretend to look out
the window.

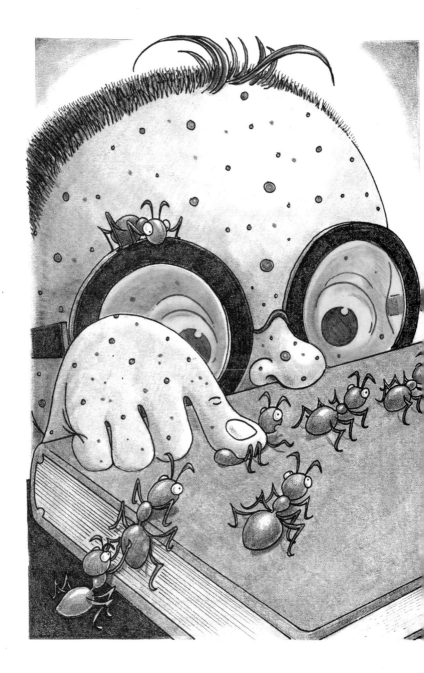

Ants

I almost forgot to write
about my pet ants!
I used to have just one.
Then I found out that
where there's one ant,
there's usually a lot more!

I feed my pet ants
little bits of candy.
I haven't told my mom
about them yet.
I'm not sure
she'd like them very much.
They are walking
all over my room!

My Cake

Guess what?
Tomorrow is my birthday!
My dad is baking a cake.
I'm helping him stir the batter.
Mmmm, it's very sweet.

I can't wait until tomorrow
to eat the cake!

My book is almost done.
I've written about lots of things—
things I saw through my glasses.

I've written about candy,
music, and dragons.
And sisters, tree houses,
and ants, too.

I've also written about
my sweet tooth.
I love cake!

I wonder what I'll write about in my next book!